The LAST FIREHAWK

Lullaby Lake

by
Katrina Charman

BRANCHES

SCHOLASTIC INC.

The LAST FIREHAWK

Read All the Books

1. THE LAST FIREHAWK: The Ember Stone — by Katrina Charman, illustrated by Jeremy Norton

2. THE LAST FIREHAWK: The Crystal Caverns — by Katrina Charman, illustrated by Jeremy Norton

3. THE LAST FIREHAWK: The Whispering Oak — by Katrina Charman, illustrated by Jeremy Norton

4. THE LAST FIREHAWK: Lullaby Lake — by Katrina Charman, illustrated by Jeremy Norton

More books coming soon!

Table of Contents

For Maddie, Piper, and Riley. —KC
Thank you to my parents, who showed me the value of art. —JN

Copyright © 2018 by Katrina Charman
Illustrations by Jeremy Norton copyright © 2018 by Scholastic Inc.

All rights reserved. Published by Scholastic Inc., *Publishers since 1920.*
SCHOLASTIC, BRANCHES, and associated logos are trademarks and/or registered trademarks of Scholastic Inc.

The publisher does not have any control over and does not assume any responsibility for author or third-party websites or their content.

No part of this publication may be reproduced, stored in a retrieval system, or transmitted in any form or by any means, electronic, mechanical, photocopying, recording, or otherwise, without written permission of the publisher. For information regarding permission, write to Scholastic Inc., Attention: Permissions Department, 557 Broadway, New York, NY 10012.

This book is a work of fiction. Names, characters, places, and incidents are either the product of the author's imagination or are used fictitiously, and any resemblance to actual persons, living or dead, business establishments, events, or locales is entirely coincidental.

Library of Congress Cataloging-in-Publication Data
Names: Charman, Katrina, author. | Norton, Jeremy, illustrator.
Title: Lullaby Lake / by Katrina Charman ; illustrated by Jeremy Norton.
Description: First edition. | New York, NY : Branches/Scholastic Inc., 2018.
| Series: The last firehawk ; 4 | Summary: Their magical map is leading Tag, Skyla, and Blaze closer and closer to The Shadowlands, Thorn's territory—but now the Ember Stone has fallen into the well-named Lullaby Lake, which is defended by fairies who sing intruders to sleep, and the friends must figure out a way to convince the "nixies" to help them retrieve it before Thorn gets his claws on it.
Identifiers: LCCN 2017037059| ISBN 9781338122671 (pbk.) |
ISBN 9781338122718 (hardcover)
Subjects: LCSH: Owls—Juvenile fiction. | Squirrels—Juvenile fiction. |
Animals, Mythical—Juvenile fiction. | Magic—Juvenile fiction. |
Fairies—Juvenile fiction. | Quests (Expeditions)—Juvenile fiction. |
Adventure stories. | CYAC: Owls--Fiction. | Squirrels—Fiction. | Animals, Mythical—Fiction. | Magic—Fiction. | Adventure and adventurers—Fiction. | Fantasy. | GSAFD: Adventure fiction. | LCGFT: Action and adventure fiction.
Classification: LCC PZ7.1.C495 Lu 2018 | DDC [Fic]—dc23
LC record available at https://lccn.loc.gov/2017037059

10 9 8 7 6 5 4 3 2 1   18 19 20 21 22

Printed in China   38
First edition, August 2018
Edited by Katie Carella
Book design by Maria Mercado

~ INTRODUCTION ~

In the enchanted land of Perodia, lies Valor Wood—a forest filled with magic and light. There, a wise owl named Grey leads the Owls of Valor. These brave warriors protect the creatures of the wood. But a darkness is spreading across Perodia, and the forest's magic and light are fading away . . .

A powerful old vulture called Thorn controls The Shadow—a dark magic. Whenever The Shadow appears, Thorn and his army of orange-eyed spies are nearby. Thorn will not stop until Perodia is destroyed.

Tag, a small barn owl, and his friends Skyla and Blaze, the last firehawk, have found three pieces of the magical Ember Stone. This stone may be strong enough to stop Thorn once and for all. But there are more pieces to be found. Thorn and his spies are also searching for the stone—and for Blaze. The friends' journey continues . . .

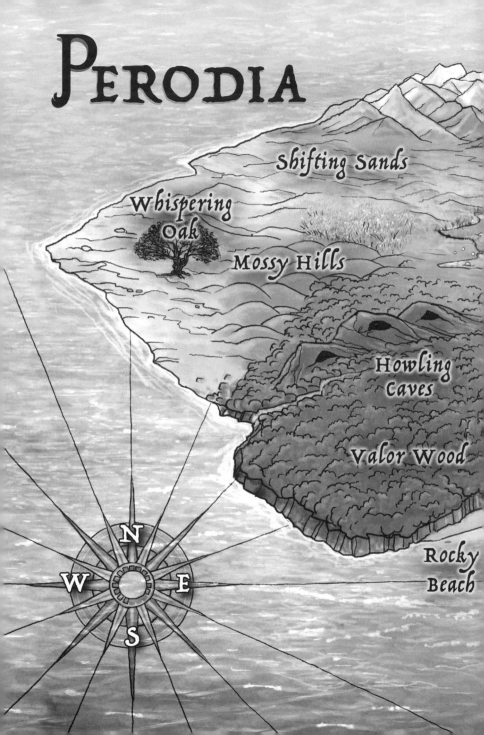

Crystal Caverns

Jagged Mountains

Bubbling
Bog

Lullaby Lake

The Shadowlands

Blue Bay

Fire Island

PERODIA

TO LULLABY LAKE!

Tag and his friends Skyla and Blaze stood at the bottom of the Mossy Hills. The area around them was dry. The trees and bushes were brown from where Thorn and The Shadow had destroyed them.

"We must journey to Lullaby Lake for the next piece of the Ember Stone," Tag said, looking at the bright spot on the magical map Grey had given them.

Skyla pointed to a dark brown area on the map. It was in between the Mossy Hills and the lake. "What's that?" she asked.

Tag read the map. "The Bubbling Bog."

Blaze leaned over Tag's shoulder. Tag couldn't believe how tall his friend had grown. She towered over him and Skyla, and she had learned lots of new words. She also had amazing powers—firepower, super-strong wings, and a loud cry that would scare away any enemy. Tag smiled. He was glad he had a firehawk on his side.

Blaze tapped her beak on the map. "Thorn!" she cried.

"Blaze is right," Skyla said. "The lake is close to The Shadowlands. That's where Thorn lives."

"We will stay as far north as we can," Tag said.

He looked at the sky, searching for The Shadow. But the sky was clear.

For now.

"We need to leave right away," Tag said. "Thorn and his spies are getting closer. And we move faster in the air, so we should fly."

Skyla nodded, climbing onto Blaze's back.

Tag rolled up the map. He put it into his sack of supplies and checked their piece of the Ember Stone. There was a sharp, jagged edge on one side of the stone. This was where another piece—or more—could fit. Each time they found a new piece, it magically joined with the others, making a larger stone.

How many more pieces are there? Tag wondered.

Blaze took to the sky.

Tag was right on her heels, heading east toward Lullaby Lake.

The friends flew as fast as they could. They were quiet, all wondering what they might find at the Bubbling Bog and beyond.

THE BUBBLING BOG

As the friends flew closer to the Bubbling Bog, their eyes began to water.

"What is that smell?" Skyla called to Tag and Blaze.

"It's the bog!" Tag replied, covering his beak with his wing.

Thick, squelchy mud stretched out as far as he could see. Every so often, a huge bubble rose up from the mud. When it popped, it let out a small cloud of smelly green gas.

"My eyes sting!" cried Blaze.

"Mine, too," Tag said, blinking to stop his eyes going blurry.

BELCH! BURP! The bog bubbled.

"We can't fly over the bog!" Skyla yelled. "Those bubbles must be filled with some kind of poison."

"Follow me!" Tag shouted. He flew north, and they landed at the edge of the Bubbling Bog.

Skyla pinched her nose. "What do we do now?"

Tag pulled out the map. "We'll have to stay to the north. It will take longer than flying over the bog, but it's the only way."

"Hurry," Blaze told her friends.

Skyla didn't wait to be told twice. She hopped onto Blaze's back, and they set off, leaving the stinky bog far behind.

They flew for hours.

Just before sundown, they reached Lullaby Lake. The air was fresh, and the water clear. They found a group of willow trees at the edge of the lake. The trees had long branches that hung to the ground.

"Look at this," Skyla said.

She moved some branches aside and disappeared behind them. Tag and Blaze followed.

"It's a secret hideout," Tag said. The branches hung low, keeping the friends hidden.

"We should set up camp here," Skyla said.

"Thorn's spies will never find us," Blaze agreed.

"Is our piece of the Ember Stone warm yet?" Skyla asked. Usually, when they were close to another piece, theirs glowed and got hotter.

Tag checked his sack. "No, it is still cold," he said.

Blaze peered out of the branches. She pointed at a small island in the middle of the lake.

"Let's check out that island," Tag said. "Maybe the next piece is over there."

"I'll stay here and make our nests for tonight," Skyla said. She picked up some thin branches and began weaving nests for them to sleep on.

Tag and Blaze flew to the island. It was covered in trees and tall grass, but there was no sign of the next piece.

"It's not here," Blaze said.

Tag checked the stone in his sack. It was cold.

The moon rose in the night sky. Tag hoped that none of Thorn's spies were watching. He didn't want them to find the next piece before he and his friends did.

Tag patted Blaze's wing. "This is a big lake," he said. "Let's head back to camp. We'll search more in the morning."

CHAPTER 3

THORN!

Tag and Blaze returned to camp as night fell.

"We should take turns keeping watch," Skyla said.

"I'll go first," Tag replied.

He set his sack down and peered through a small gap in the branches. There was no sign of Thorn's spies, but Tag knew they would show up sooner or later. They always did.

— 15 —

Tag looked at the sack. It held his dagger, the map, and their piece of the Ember Stone. It was his job to keep the sack—and his friends—safe.

Blaze and Skyla snored quietly. The branches of the willow tree kept them hidden, but an icy wind blew through the leaves. Tag shivered as the night grew colder. He wished Blaze was awake so she could light up her feathers to keep them warm.

The hours passed. Tag felt tired, but he knew he needed to stay awake. Suddenly, he noticed a black cloud creeping toward the lake.

The Shadow! Tag thought, jumping up. Flashes of lightning filled the sky.

Slowly, the leaves of the willow tree began to turn brown. They crumbled to the ground like dust . . .

A large, crooked vulture stood before him! *THORN!*

Tag squeaked. He knew he needed to grab the sack, but he couldn't move. His feathers shook with fear.

"We meet at last," Thorn hissed. An evil grin spread across the vulture's face as he reached his sharp claws toward the sack. "I think you have something that belongs to me."

Just in time, Tag snatched the sack out of Thorn's reach. Thorn snarled.

Tag pulled out his dagger, holding it with a shaky wing.

"Thorn!" Tag yelled to his friends.

In an instant, Blaze and Skyla awoke.

Skyla aimed her slingshot at Thorn's wrinkled face. "Don't move!" she shouted bravely, although her paw trembled.

Blaze spread her wings. Her feathers lit up all at once. The flames glowed red and orange in the darkness.

But Thorn did not seem afraid. "Your powers are stronger than I realized," he said. "Think how powerful we could be if we worked together."

"Never!" Blaze cried.

Quick as a flash, Thorn took another swipe at Tag's sack. His sharp claws ripped it open and the Ember Stone fell out.

"No!" Tag yelled.

Thorn scooped up the stone in his sharp claws. Then he took off—flying over the water, toward The Shadowlands.

Skyla shot acorns from shore, while Tag and Blaze chased after the vulture by air.

Blaze blasted fireballs at Thorn. One of them hit Thorn on the back. Thorn howled and dropped the Ember Stone. It fell down, down, down—

SPLASH! The stone hit the lake below.

Thorn shrieked, and the sky flashed with lightning. He swooped down to the lake's surface, but Blaze shot more fireballs at him.

Thorn shrieked again and turned to the friends.

"This isn't over!" Thorn squawked. Then he flew away, toward the dark cloud of The Shadow.

As soon as Thorn was gone, Tag soared over the surface of the water. Blaze circled above, keeping watch.

But it was too late. The Ember Stone had already sunk to the lake bottom.

Suddenly, Tag saw a zigzaggy flash of blue light in the water. Long, dark shapes surrounded the stone. And hundreds of bright orange eyes glared up at Tag.

THE LOST STONE

"**T**horn has spies in the water!" Tag shouted. "Eels!"

Blaze and Tag circled above the lake, watching the eels' flashing blue light and glowing orange eyes.

BUZZZZ! BUZZZZ!

"What's that sound?" Tag asked.

Blaze soared closer to the water.

BUZZZZ! The sound grew louder and the flashes of blue light grew brighter. Blaze dipped her beak in the lake.

"Ow!" Blaze cried, zooming up out of the water.

"They're *electric* eels!" Tag said.

Tag and Blaze headed back to shore.

"What happened out there?" Skyla asked as Blaze rubbed her beak.

"Our stone is at the bottom of the lake," Blaze said.

"And Thorn's spies are guarding it," Tag said. He put his head in his wings.

They had already come so far to find the pieces that made up their stone—traveling to Fire Island, the Crystal Caverns, and the Whispering Oak. Those three pieces had joined to make one stone, but now that stone was lost underwater.

"This is all my fault!" Tag cried. "I should have stopped Thorn from taking our stone. Now it looks like he will get our stone *and* the next piece."

Blaze stamped her feet. "No!" she cried.

Skyla turned to Tag. "It wasn't your fault Thorn stole our stone," she said. "We can get it back, I know we can."

"Peep!" Blaze agreed.

Tag smiled. "Okay," he said. "But how? If we touch the water, we'll be zapped!"

"Use a branch?" Blaze suggested.

"That won't work," Tag said. "A branch wouldn't be long enough to reach the bottom of the lake."

Skyla looked back at the willow trees. "I have an idea!" she said.

Tag and Blaze followed Skyla to camp, where she quickly got to work. She gathered one of their nests and twisted the branches and twigs and leaves together into a new shape.

"We can't go *in* the water," Skyla said, "but we can get closer to the stone by going *on* the water."

"A raft!" Tag said as he saw what his friend was making. "We can use it to float out on the lake!"

"But we still need something to reach the stone *under* the water . . ." Blaze said.

Skyla winked, then pulled down a long, sturdy branch from the tree. She twisted together some leaves to make a net and tied it to the end. When she was finished, she showed them her handiwork.

"Who wants to go fishing?" she asked.

SWEET DREAMS

Tag inspected the raft and net as the sun rose over Lullaby Lake.

"It's the perfect plan!" he said. "I'll float out to the middle of the lake and scoop up our stone."

Blaze shook her head. "I will go."

"You're too big," Tag told her. "You will sink the raft. And Skyla is afraid of the water. I'm the only one who can do it."

Blaze nodded.

"Just remember: Don't touch the water," Skyla told Tag. "You'll get zapped."

Tag looked at the blue glow coming from the surface of the lake and shivered. "Don't worry, I won't," he said.

He carefully stepped onto the raft. It was the perfect size for him. Skyla passed him the net.

Blaze guided the raft out across the lake, then flew back to shore.

Tag looked down. The water was clear. He could see brightly colored fish swimming among the reeds.

As the raft neared the center of the lake, Tag spotted the long, bright blue shapes of the electric eels. Their orange eyes glowed beneath the water as they circled a purple light.

I can see our stone! Tag thought. *And it's glowing!*

Tag dipped the net into the water. The eels buzzed, shooting out flashes of light. But Tag stayed focused. He guided the net closer to the glowing piece on the lake bottom.

Suddenly, a hundred sparkling, golden lights appeared just beneath the surface! Tag tightened his grip on the net, wishing he had his dagger. But then a soft, gentle song floated up from the water. It sounded like tinkling raindrops. It was the most beautiful sound Tag had ever heard. The lights surrounded the eels and Tag's raft.

The eels drifted away.

Tag lay down on the raft as he listened to the lullaby. He looked up at the puffy white clouds in the sky. The net slipped from his wing onto the raft.

Soon, he forgot he was looking for anything at all and fell fast asleep.

CHAPTER

6

NOT AGAIN!

Tag woke with a start. The sun was high in the sky, which meant he'd slept for hours. He was still on the raft, but back on the shore. He couldn't remember what he had been doing. He yawned and gazed across Lullaby Lake.

Then he saw his net beside him, and he remembered.

Tag frowned. *How did I end up back here? And where are Skyla and Blaze?* he thought. *Oh no! I hope Thorn didn't return while I was sleeping!*

Tag flew along the shore, looking for his friends.

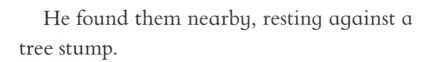

He found them nearby, resting against a tree stump.

Blaze was in such a deep sleep that Tag had to shout to wake her. "Blaze!"

Blaze jumped up. Her magical feathers lit up with tiny orange and yellow flames. "PEEP!"

"It's me!" Tag said, backing away from Blaze's fiery wings.

Blaze's feathers returned to normal.

Skyla rubbed her eyes. "Tag," she said. "What happened?"

"I'm not sure. One minute I was in the middle of the lake looking into the water . . . The next, I was fast asleep. I woke up back on shore," Tag said. "Did you two see what happened?"

Skyla and Blaze looked at each other. "We fell asleep, too," Skyla admitted.

"I'm *still* sleepy," Blaze said.

Tag sighed. "I guess we didn't get much sleep last night. And we traveled a long way yesterday," he said.

But how did my raft get back to shore? Tag wondered.

"Did you see our stone?" Blaze asked.

Tag shook his head and frowned. He thought he had seen their stone in the water, but now he wasn't so sure. He headed to the raft. "Let's try again. I'm not tired anymore."

Blaze guided the raft back to the center of the lake. Tag looked over the edge, searching for their stone. The eels' blue light moved around him.

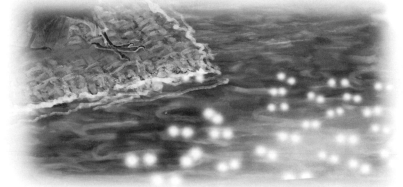

Again, the water sparkled with a hundred tiny, golden lights, and the eels drifted away. Then Tag heard the same soft music sailing across the water.

I've heard that song before, Tag thought, as he fell into a deep sleep.

THE LULLABY

T ag awoke and rubbed his eyes. *Something strange is definitely going on!* he thought.

Blaze and Skyla were asleep again.

"Blaze! Skyla! Wake up!" Tag yelled.

"Huh?!" Skyla jumped up and grabbed her slingshot.

"Did you see the stone?" Blaze asked.

"No," Tag said. "I saw golden lights in the water again and heard a strange song. Then I fell asleep."

Skyla's eyes grew wide. "I heard music, too!"

"So did I!" Blaze added.

"I'm not sure what's happening. But we have to keep trying to reach our stone," Tag said. "Thorn will be back soon."

HAAAA! HAAAA! HAAAA!

The friends heard a slow laugh.

"Look up!" Blaze said.

A hairy, gray sloth was hanging from the tree branches above.

"You can keep trying," the sloth said slowly. "But you will just end up right back where you started."

Skyla aimed her slingshot at the sloth. "Do you work for Thorn?" she asked.

Tag peered at the sloth's eyes. They were brown. "He's not one of Thorn's spies," he whispered.

Skyla lowered her slingshot. "I'm Skyla. This is Tag and Blaze."

"I'm Stanley," the sloth said. "Pleased to meet you."

"So, Stanley, what makes you think we'll end up back here again?" Skyla asked.

"You are being tricked by the nixies," Stanley said.

"What are nixies?" Blaze asked.

"Water fairies," Stanley replied. "They protect the lake."

"We don't want to harm the lake. We are searching for something that fell in there," Skyla explained. "We need to get it back right away."

Tag remembered seeing their stone glowing on the lake bottom.

Their stone glowed when the next piece was nearby. *That must mean that the new piece was also underwater!* He turned to the sloth and asked, "Was there a magical stone in the lake before we arrived? Is that what the nixies are protecting?"

Stanley shook his head slowly. "All I know is that the nixies sing when they sense danger. Your stone will be safe in the lake. Nobody can resist their song—not even Thorn's spies."

The lake began to sparkle. A lullaby drifted across the water.

Stanley yawned. "Not even me . . ." he added.

Tag's feathers drooped. *Now we'll never get our stone back. And we'll never find the next piece . . .*

The friends gave into the music and their eyes closed.

ATTACK!

Tag paced back and forth.

"There *has* to be a way for us to reach the stone without falling asleep," he said. "We need to block out the nixie's music."

"What if the eels have our stone by now?" Skyla asked.

"I don't think they can reach it either,"
Tag said. "You heard what Stanley said—
even Thorn's spies cannot resist the nixies'
song."

"Thorn will be back soon," Skyla said,
pointing to the dark cloud of The Shadow in
the distance.

"I won't let him sneak up on us this time,"
Tag said.

Just then, the friends heard the flap of
many wings overhead. Huge, striped
creatures circled in the air, snapping their
long, sharp beaks.

CLACK! CLACK! CLACK!

"Tiger bats!" Tag shouted as he pulled out his dagger.

The friends ducked behind a willow tree.

Suddenly, the lake lit up with hundreds of golden lights. It sparkled brightly as the tiger bats swooped low across the water.

"I don't think the tiger bats are looking for us . . ." Tag whispered.

"Then what are they doing?" Skyla asked, as she watched the bats land on the shore nearby.

One of the tiger bats held something small and bright in its long beak. It shone gold in the darkness.

The friends crept closer for a better look. A tiny scream came from the glowing thing.

Tag gasped. "I think they've captured a nixie!"

NOVA

"**W**e have to rescue the nixie!" Tag said. He gripped his dagger and rushed toward the tiger bats.

Skyla followed, shooting acorns. **BONK!** She hit the tiger bat holding the nixie, and the tiny fairy fell to the ground.

Blaze let out a loud cry: **SKRAAA!**

Thorn's spies covered their ears. Blaze threw small flames at the tiger bats. They squawked and took to the sky.

"That will teach them not to mess with us!" Skyla laughed.

Tag flapped over to the nixie. Her eyes were closed and her crumpled wings were wet.

"Oh no!" Blaze cried.

"Is she okay?" Skyla asked.

Tag bent over the little nixie. She wasn't much bigger than a butterfly. Her face was pale, and her bright light blinked on and off.

Blaze gave a sad peep as Tag picked up the nixie.

Skyla put her paw on Tag's shoulder. "Thorn must have wanted to try to use a nixie to get to the stone," she said.

Suddenly, one of the nixie's eyes opened, then the other. She sat up.

"Are they gone?" the nixie asked.

Tag nodded.

"Phew!" the nixie said with a grin. She stood up and flapped her wings. Her body glowed golden and bright again. "Thanks for saving me!"

"You're welcome," Tag said, smiling. "Any enemy of the tiger bats is a friend of ours."

The nixie looked up at the three friends towering over her. Her eyes grew wide when she spotted Blaze.

"That's Blaze," Tag told her. "She is a firehawk. I'm Tag, and this is Skyla." He held out a wing to shake the nixie's tiny hand.

"I'm Nova," the nixie said. She frowned at Blaze. "A firehawk? I thought you were all in hiding."

Blaze opened her beak to ask the nixie what she meant, but—

Wings flapped overhead.

"The tiger bats are back!" Skyla yelled.

"Run!" Tag said, heading for the trees.

UNDERWATER MAGIC

Tag, Skyla, Blaze, and Nova hid in the willow trees.

CLACK! CLACK! CLACK!

Tag caught his breath as he listened to the tiger bats' beaks snapping in the sky above.

After a while, the tiger bats flapped away.

"Phew!" Nova sighed. She smiled at her new friends. "So, what brings you to Lullaby Lake?" she asked, fluttering over Tag's head.

"We are on a long journey, in search of all the pieces of the Ember Stone," Tag told her. "Our magical map led us here for the next piece, but Thorn showed up."

"He tried to steal our piece, but he dropped it into the lake," Blaze explained.

"So *that's* why Thorn came to our lake!" Nova said. "We knew something strange was happening when those electric eels magically appeared."

"I'm sorry," Tag replied.

"We're trying to get our stone back. But we haven't been able to get past Thorn's spies—the electric eels," Skyla said.

"And you and your friends keep putting us to sleep," Tag added.

Nova's face turned pink. "I'm sorry," she said. "But we have to protect *our* piece of the Ember Stone." She clapped her hand over her mouth.

Then I did see our stone glow! Tag thought. *It glowed because it was near the nixies' piece of the stone!*

"You have the next piece! Where is it?" Tag asked, his eyes wide.

"My father will explain everything," Nova said, pointing to the water. "I will take you to him—at the bottom of the lake."

"I can't swim!" Skyla cried.

"You don't need to swim," Nova said with a smile.

"What about the eels? And the tiger bats? I'm sure they're still nearby," Tag said.

Nova's wings glowed. "Leave them to me."

She flew into a tree and picked a handful of soft blossoms.

"Put these in your ears," she said.

Tag, Blaze, and Skyla placed the fluffy blossoms in their ears. Tag watched as Nova opened her mouth and started singing. Her wings glowed brighter.

The tiger bats came out from beneath a willow tree across the lake, as though in a trance. Then they fell to the ground, sleeping soundly.

Nova stopped singing and waved at the friends to remove the blossoms.

"Follow me," Nova said, flying toward the water.

Nova's wings glowed a soft pink color. She held out her hands, and tiny, glittery sparkles rose to make four shiny bubbles. The bubbles grew and grew until they were as big as Blaze.

Nova pointed to the bubbles. "These will take us beneath the water."

Tag scratched his head. "How?" he asked.

BLOOP!

"Like that!" The nixie laughed at Blaze, who had stepped inside a bubble. Then she stepped inside one, too.

"Peep!" Blaze smiled.

Tag took a step forward. **BLOOP!**

"What if my bubble pops underwater?" Skyla called from inside hers.

"It won't," the nixie promised.

Tag's tummy flopped as his bubble rose into the air.

The friends floated over the lake, then slowly sank beneath the water.

THE NIXIE KINGDOM

The lake was deeper than Tag had thought. He felt he was sinking to the bottom like a rock. But really, he was floating down, down, down. Tiny, golden lights surrounded them, guiding them to the bottom of the lake.

63

Tag looked over at his friends. Their bubbles were full of air—so they could breathe underwater! Colorful fish swam in and out of weeds. Blaze waved at one fish, but it ignored her and swam past.

Skyla did not look so happy. Her tail flicked back and forth as she held her paws over her eyes.

"Electric eels!" Blaze cried out suddenly, pointing.

Tag could see orange eyes peering out from the weeds.

Nova waved at Tag and his friends to put the blossoms back in their ears. Then she opened her mouth. She was singing again. The eels quickly drifted away and the friends removed the blossoms.

On the lake bottom, Tag spotted another glimmering light. It sparkled gold and silver through the water.

The light grew bigger and bigger as the friends' bubbles floated closer to it. Soon, their rainbow-colored bubbles floated above a giant bubble at the very bottom of Lullaby Lake. There was a huge palace in the middle. It glittered silver beneath the dome.

"*This* is where you live?" Tag asked, his eyes wide.

"Welcome to the Nixie Kingdom!" Nova said.

CHAPTER 12

A ROYAL WELCOME

All at once, the four friends' bubbles sank into the large dome over the Nixie Kingdom. They floated to the ground. Then—

POP!

Tag, Skyla, Blaze, and Nova's bubbles burst, sprinkling glitter all around.

Skyla was still covering her eyes.

"Skyla, look at this amazing underwater world," Tag said.

Skyla uncovered her eyes and gasped. "Your home is beautiful, Nova!" she said.

"It's amazing!" Blaze agreed.

Tag stared at the underwater kingdom. There were tiny white houses and a tall ivory palace in the center. Everywhere Tag looked, he saw nixies fluttering around and having fun.

The bubble dome was see-through, and Tag could see fish and plants in the lake, too.

Some nixies nearby started singing.

Blaze covered her ears. "No more sleep!" she cried.

"Don't worry," Nova said. "Only a special magical lullaby can make you fall asleep."

Skyla put her hands on her hips. "Why did you make us fall asleep before?" she asked.

"Did you think we were Thorn's spies?" Tag added.

"We were told not to let *anyone* near the lake. It is too dangerous. Thorn and his spies were getting too close to—" Nova paused. "My father will explain. Follow me."

They followed Nova to the tall, sparkling doors of the palace.

Two nixies wearing silver armor opened the doors. "Welcome home, Princess Nova," the guards said.

Tag's jaw dropped. "Princess?" he asked.

"I should have told you after you saved me from the tiger bats," Nova said.

"Tiger bats?" a voice boomed.

A nixie wearing a shiny crown flew toward them inside the great hall. His long, golden robe hung to the floor behind him.

Nova blushed. "The tiger bats sneaked up on me, Father," she said. "But my new friends saved me. This is Tag, Blaze, and Skyla."

The king flew up to them. "Thank you for saving my daughter." The king smiled. "I am King Nidus."

The king looked at each of the friends. His eyes widened when they stopped on Blaze. "A firehawk!" he cried, bowing to Blaze. "I thought you were all gone."

"I am the last firehawk," Blaze told the king.

The king raised his hands. Light sparkled above them, filling the air with glittery magic.

A long table appeared in the middle of the great hall. It was covered with mountains of food.

"We will have a feast in your honor!" the king told Blaze. "And to thank you all for saving Nova."

Skyla grinned. "I'm starving!" she said.

Tag elbowed his friend. "Thank you, Your Majesty," he said to the king.

Tag, Skyla, and Blaze bowed. Then they rushed over to the table.

Skyla grabbed a handful of grapes while Tag dunked his beak into a bubbling bowl of bright green soup. More nixies joined them, eating and chatting.

"So what brings you to my kingdom?" King Nidus asked.

Tag turned to the king. "We are searching for all the pieces of the Ember Stone."

The king's smile faded.

"We need to complete the Ember Stone in order to use it to defeat Thorn," Tag went on. "Without it, we cannot save Perodia. Yesterday, our own piece fell in the lake. And Nova said that you have one of your own, too. We were hoping you could help us?"

The great hall fell silent as the king flew up into Tag's face. He scowled at Tag. "Those stones are ours," the king said. "You cannot have them."

KING NIDUS

Nova flew over to her father.

"Please, Father—Tag, Skyla, and Blaze saved me," she said. "You can trust them."

The king's eyebrows knotted together as he thought hard. "Fine. Your friends may take *their* piece of the Ember Stone. But the firehawks hid these pieces across Perodia to keep them safe. And they trusted us to guard *our* piece," he told her. "That one must stay here at the palace."

"But, Father," Nova said, "I am sure Thorn's spies have told him everything by now. That means Thorn knows there are two pieces of the stone in our lake. He will send even more spies. They already tried to kidnap me today. I'm sure that was just the beginning. Thorn will not stop until both pieces are his."

Skyla stepped forward. "Can't you just put Thorn to sleep if he tries to enter the lake?" she asked.

Nova frowned. "Thorn's powerful dark magic allows him to resist our magic lullaby."

Tag turned to the king. "If you give *us* both pieces, then maybe Thorn will leave *you* alone?" he said.

The king shook his head again. "Thorn will never stop. But you cannot have our piece," he said. "Now follow me. I will take you to yours."

The friends followed Nova and King Nidus down a spiral staircase, then along a hallway that led to a tall, silver door. The king pulled out a golden key and slotted it into the keyhole.

When the door opened, a bright purple light shone out.

THE NEXT PIECE

Blaze hopped up and down. "The Ember Stone!" she said.

A glass case sat on a table in the middle of the room. It held a small, jagged piece of the stone.

"This is the new piece we've been searching for!" Tag exclaimed.

"As I've already told you, you may not have it," King Nidus said firmly. "I promised the firehawks 1 would guard our piece with my life."

Blaze stepped forward. "I *am* a firehawk," she said. "The Ember Stone belongs with me."

The king paced up and down, thinking about what Blaze had said. Tag could tell that the king felt a duty to keep his piece of the Ember Stone.

"Um . . ." Skyla said, breaking the silence. "Where is *our* stone?"

Nova opened a large wooden chest from beneath the table. Then she helped her father lift out a crystal box bigger than the two of them.

Both pieces were glowing brightly from being so close to each other.

"When your stone dropped into the lake, we brought it here," Nova told them.

"Thank you for keeping it safe," Tag said.

Skyla gently nudged Tag. "We really need to put these stones together to see if we have all the pieces now," she whispered.

Tag nodded, then turned to the nixie king. "King Nidus, I have an idea. I think we can prove to you that these two pieces are meant to be together—and that Blaze was meant to have them."

The king frowned. "How?" he asked.

Tag pointed at the glass case. "Let Blaze hold the stones."

The king shook his head hard. "They are very hot! Our piece started to glow when your piece was brought into our kingdom. We are using our strongest magic just to keep them from burning down the palace," he told them.

"The stones can't hurt me," Blaze said.

"Pieces of the Ember Stone glow when they are close to one another—or to Blaze," Skyla explained.

The king lifted the cover off the glass case, as Tag opened the crystal box.

Warm purple light filled the room.

Blaze lifted the smaller piece and placed it next to their stone on the table.

Both pieces began to shake. Then a loud humming sound filled the room as they wobbled across the table toward each other. With a burst of bright purple light, they joined together and became one stone.

"Look!" Tag cried, pointing to a small jagged space at the edge of the stone. "There is only one piece left to find!"

Blaze and Skyla jumped up and down excitedly.

King Nidus waved his hand in the air, leaving a trail of glittery dust. The stone rose and floated over to Blaze.

"You are right," King Nidus said. "I see now that the stone belongs with you. I trust that you will keep it safe."

"We will," Blaze promised.

Blaze placed the glowing stone into Tag's sack, but it fell out through the hole Thorn's sharp claw had made.

"I'll fix that," said Nova. She sprinkled golden dust over the sack and repaired the hole. Then the stone floated back into the sack.

"Thanks," said Tag.

The king smiled. "I never thought I'd see a firehawk," he said. "It has been so nice to meet you—all of you. Thank you again for saving my daughter."

The friends bowed to the king.

"Sleep in the palace tonight," the king continued. "It will be safer for you to leave in the morning."

"Thank you," Tag replied. "We will leave at sunrise."

HEADING HOME

The next morning, sunlight shone through the window of their bedroom in the Nixie Palace.

"Time to go," Tag said. "We need to hurry in case Thorn or his spies are waiting for us."

Skyla held up her slingshot. "We'll be ready for them if they are."

Blaze's feathers flashed brightly. "I'm ready," she said.

Nova met the friends outside the palace. "Are you sure you don't want to stay with us?" Nova asked. "You would be safe here."

Tag shook his head. "We have to find the last piece of the Ember Stone," he said. "It's the only way to save Perodia."

"I understand," Nova said. She took a deep breath. "Ready?" she asked.

Tag nodded.

Nova's wings glowed a soft pink color. She held out her hands and glitter filled the air, turning into three large bubbles.

Tag, Skyla, and Blaze stepped into their bubbles with a loud **BLOOP, BLOOP, BLOOP**! They waved to Nova as the shiny bubbles floated gently upward.

"Good luck!" Nova called. "If you need help, just call into the shell." She pointed at a large shell that magically appeared at Tag's feet. He picked it up.

Tag put the magic shell inside his sack.

Hundreds of tiny, golden lights floated around the three friends, pushing them all the way to the surface.

POP! Their bubbles burst on the shore, sprinkling glitter all around.

Tag glanced at the sky. It was clear. There was no sign of Thorn or his spies.

"Where to next?" Skyla asked.

Tag pulled out the map and set the stone on top of it. A small, shining dot appeared on the map. Blaze gasped as she peered over Tag's shoulder.

"Valor Wood!" Skyla cried.

"The next piece is back where we started," Tag said. He looked at his friends. "We're going home. It is time to stop Thorn once and for all."

ABOUT THE AUTHOR

KATRINA CHARMAN has wanted to be a children's book writer ever since she was eleven, when her teacher asked her class to write an epilogue to Roald Dahl's *Matilda*. Katrina's teacher thought her writing was good enough to send to Roald Dahl himself! Sadly, she never got a reply, but this experience ignited her love of reading and writing. Katrina lives in England with her husband and three daughters. The Last Firehawk is her first early chapter book series in the US.

ABOUT THE ILLUSTRATOR

JEREMY NORTON is an accomplished illustrator and artist who uses digital media to develop images and ideas on screen with light. He was an imaginative and prolific artist as a child, and he still tries to convey that same sense of wonder in his work. Jeremy lives in Spain. The Last Firehawk is his first early chapter book series with Scholastic.

The LAST FIREHAWK
Lullaby Lake

Questions and Activities

1. **W**hy do Tag and his friends fly *around* the Bubbling Bog rather than flying *over* it?

2. **M**ost of this book takes place at Lullaby Lake. What is a lullaby? (Use a dictionary to check your answer!) Why does the lake have this name?

3. **N**ova gives Tag and his friends two things to help them reach the underwater Nixie Kingdom. What are these things? How does each item help them travel there safely?

4. **W**hy does King Nidus not want to give up his piece of the Ember Stone? Reread page 79.

5. **S**kyla uses natural materials such as leaves and twigs to build a raft. What could you create using the same materials? Draw a picture of your invention.